D0522074

EUROPE AND
THE NEAR EAST
IN 1095

Christian
Muslim

EUROPE

Constantinople

Jerusalem

EGYPT

NORTH AFRICA

This map shows the lands controlled by Christian and Muslim rulers at the start of the crusades.

CRUSADERS

Rob Lloyd Jones

History consultant: Jonathan Harris,
Royal Holloway, University of London

Reading consultant: Alison Kelly, Roehampton University

Contents

CHAPTER 1

The Holy City

To Christians in the Middle Ages, the ancient city of Jerusalem was the most sacred place in the world. At its heart sat the Church of the Holy Sepulchre – the site where Jesus was said to have risen to heaven. Each year, hundreds of Christians made long hard journeys, known as pilgrimages, to reach this sacred shrine.

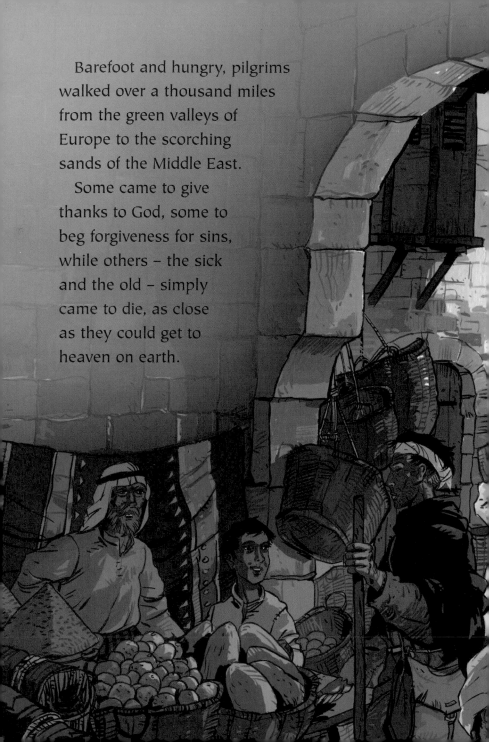

Barefoot and hungry, pilgrims walked over a thousand miles from the green valleys of Europe to the scorching sands of the Middle East.

Some came to give thanks to God, some to beg forgiveness for sins, while others – the sick and the old – simply came to die, as close as they could get to heaven on earth.

But Jerusalem wasn't only sacred to Christians.
Followers of the Islamic faith, the Muslims, believed
that Muhammad, the founder of their religion,
also rose to heaven from within the city's walls.
Ever since the year 638, when Jerusalem had been
captured by the Arabs, it had been under Islamic
control. Each day, thousands of Muslims gathered
to worship at the Dome of the Rock, a golden-
domed temple in the middle of the city.

Despite their differences, Muslims and Christians
– as well as Jews and others – lived in harmony in
the city and the area around it, which was
known as the Holy Land.

Then, at the end of the 11th century, a group of fierce Muslim warriors, the Seljuk Turks, swept from Central Asia.

The Seljuks conquered Jerusalem, and then marched within a hundred miles of a great Christian city in the north – Constantinople.

Desperate to stop them, the Christian ruler in Constantinople, Alexius Commenus, sent a plea for help to the Pope in Rome. All he wanted was a few hundred knights to help defend his lands. What he got was something very different...

CHAPTER 2

Call to arms

"A grave report has come from the land of Jerusalem…"

Pope Urban II paused for a moment, letting the crowd consider his words. Almost everyone in the French town of Clermont had gathered outside the cathedral to hear his speech. Few of them had even seen a bishop before, let alone the Pope – the leader of the Christian world. He had come here all the way from Rome, so the crowd were eager to hear what he had to say.

"Muslim armies," the Pope continued, "have invaded Jerusalem. They are slaughtering Christians, destroying churches, and laying waste to the kingdom of God."

The crowd gasped, horrified by the image of the Holy City destroyed by Saracens, the name they used to describe Muslims. In fact, neither Jerusalem nor the Christians living there had been affected much by the Seljuk conquest of the area. But the Pope wanted people to believe otherwise.

For him, the appeal for help from Constantinople had come at a perfect time. The Pope didn't just want to help the Christian ruler there – he wanted to capture Jerusalem and all of the Holy Land from the Muslims. To do so, he needed an army.

"Christians of Europe," the Pope urged, "you
have a sworn duty to protect the Holy City. You
must unite in a war to reclaim Jerusalem from the
Saracens."

The crowd stood in stunned silence. Then one of
the bishops among them stepped forward and
kneeled before the Pope. "I will go," he declared.
"I will march to Jerusalem."

Suddenly, several others in the crowd raised
their hands, cheering, "March to Jerusalem!
March to Jerusalem!"

Dozens more joined in, then hundreds. The whole crowd surged forward, chanting together, "God wills it! God wills it!"

The Pope raised his hands, shouting above their cheers. "It is, indeed, God's will," he yelled, "and let those words be your war cry when you meet the enemy!"

It was November 27, 1095, and the Pope had just launched a Holy War.

CHAPTER 3

False start

News of the Pope's speech spread fast. Soon all of Europe was gripped by a religious frenzy. "Saracens have invaded Jerusalem!" people shouted in the streets. "March to reclaim the Holy City!"

Priests shouted the message from pulpits, while the Pope himself journeyed through France, telling everyone about the campaign.

In Italy and Germany, too, thousands of people stitched red crosses onto their clothes, a sign that they would march to Jerusalem. From this cross they took their name – crusaders.

15

To most knights, the lure of the crusade was irresistible. These men were the sons of wealthy nobles, who had trained since childhood to fight. Usually, though, they had to pray for months to ask God's forgiveness for sins they committed on the battlefield. But the crusade was different – protecting the Holy Land was their religious duty. In his speech at Clermont, the Pope had promised that whatever sins they committed on this Holy War would be forgiven. People even believed that anyone who killed a Saracen would gain a place in heaven.

Even so, few knights actually looked forward to the journey. The 3,000-mile march to the Holy Land would be filled with dangers. There were no maps or guides, and nobody knew anything about the enemies they might face.

The expedition would be expensive, too. Each knight had to raise huge sums of money just to afford the weapons and supplies he would need. The planning and preparations would take months.

But for poor people who wanted to join the crusade, there was no reason to wait. Life for them was terribly hard. Rats and fleas spread diseases in crowded streets, floods and frosts brought crop failure and, each year, thousands of parents watched as their children died of starvation. Many of them saw the crusade as a holy adventure that would, somehow, lead them to better lives in the east.

Thousands took vows to 'fight for God's cause' and wore the red cross of the crusaders. Others branded the cross on their skin with hot irons. Soon, 100,000 of them were ready to march to Jerusalem.

In the spring of 1096, the 'Peasants' Crusade', as it later became known, set off. Most of the crusaders came from northern France and Germany, although thousands more joined as the group made its way through the forests and valleys of western Europe.

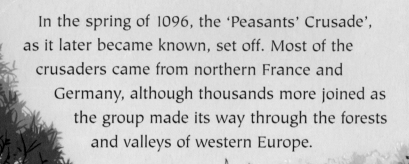

It was a march unlike anything anyone had ever seen. But it was also unplanned, unorganized, and unprepared. Few had thought about how they would actually reach Jerusalem, much less how they would conquer the city when they got there.

Most of them just believed God would lead them to victory. They had no food, no money, and no idea how hard the journey would be. Soon it began to show.

After a month of walking, the crusading hordes were stick-thin, burned by the sun and exhausted. Weakened by hunger, thirst and foul weather, thousands died and thousands more turned back home. Now their desperation boiled into anger. Reaching Hungary, one mob began looting shops and houses, killing anyone who blocked their path.

In the city of Semlin, in Hungary, another group killed 4,000 Jews, and in Belgrade they set fire to half the city. Few of the crusaders even seemed interested in reaching Jerusalem any more.

When they reached Constantinople, the Christian emperor there was horrified. He had expected an army of knights to help fight the Turks. Instead, he was greeted by a mob of unruly peasants. Desperate to get rid of them, he gave them supplies, and they continued their march into Turkish lands, attacking more and more villages as they went.

But the crusaders' fate was already sealed. Taking shelter inside an abandoned castle, they suddenly found themselves surrounded by Turkish troops. Furious at the mob's attacks on Muslim towns, the Turks showed no mercy. Almost every crusader was killed.

The Peasants' Crusade was a disaster. Of the 100,000 men and women who left Europe, only 3,000 survived. They made their way to Constantinople to join a new army that was arriving from the west. Once again, tens of thousands of Christians were setting out to liberate Jerusalem. But, this time, they weren't peasants...

CHAPTER 4

The knights' crusade

The army of crusader knights reached the edge of Europe in the summer of 1096, less than a year after the Pope's speech at Clermont. Camped outside Constantinople, the 40,000-strong force was an incredible sight. Each knight had brought his own foot soldiers, wagons loaded with weapons of war, and animals laden with supplies.

With them were 60,000 other pilgrims, including servants, cooks, and even the knights' own families. Banners flew above them, minstrels danced around them, and priests prayed for their safe passage to Jerusalem.

The vast force remained at Constantinople for several months, gathering supplies and planning their route south. Then, in the spring of 1097, they set off.

The crusaders' journey was slow from the start. The great train of carts and animals strained with the weight of supplies, and knights in heavy chain mail struggled under the scorching sun. Simply moving such a vast army from its camp took three whole days.

Meeting in their camp at night, the crusader leaders – princes and lords from all over Europe – decided to split their forces, with one half marching a day ahead of the other. They hoped to make the army faster. But they had just made it weaker.

As the first half of the army approached the Turkish town of Dorylaeum on July 1, horns began to echo from the hills around them. Suddenly, 30,000 Saracen horsemen charged into the valley. Moving with amazing speed, the attackers surrounded the knights, striking blows with arrows and spears.

Outnumbered, the crusaders' only chance was to huddle together in a circle. Led by a skilled Italian commander named Bohemond of Taranto, the knights formed a shield around the women

and children, protecting them against the swarming horsemen. "Stand fast together!" they screamed. "Stand fast together!"

Five terrible hours passed as the crusaders struggled to hold out against the enemy. Occasionally, a pack of Saracen horsemen tore through their lines, only to be fought off by the knights' shields and swords. Bombarded with arrows and spears, hundreds fell dead. But still the line held. Then, just after midday, the second half of the crusader army finally appeared at the edge of the valley. Seeing the other crusaders surrounded, they raced into battle.

The Saracens, who fought in light tunics and skirts, were no match for the knights in their heavy chain mail. Their battle style relied on speed and surprise rather than strength and numbers. So, instead of fighting the crusaders, they retreated, poisoning wells and burning crops along their enemy's route eastwards.

Soon, the crusaders began to suffer. Their journey now took them around the southern edge of a barren plateau in central Turkey. All around them, the land was cracked and lifeless. Starved of water, their horses dropped dead on the roadside. At night, their camps were plagued with venomous snakes and spiders. Eventually, hundreds of crusaders were dying each day, their bodies simply left buried along the way.

Many crusaders became so demoralized, they began to argue among themselves. Some chose to abandon the march to Jerusalem altogether, capturing smaller towns along the way instead.

Others attacked the city of Antioch, in Syria, where they rested and gathered supplies. But, even here, they continued to suffer, ravaged by deadly plagues and even an earthquake. By the time they left the city in January 1099, their army numbered less than 15,000, with only 1,300 knights. But now – finally – the road to Jerusalem lay open before them.

CHAPTER 5

The siege of Jerusalem

The crusaders stared at the city shimmering in the distance. At first, many thought it was just a mirage. But, as they got closer, the domes and walls grew clearer, and they knew they had arrived. After three years of terrible suffering, they had reached the Holy City.

But, even as they celebrated, many of them feared for the task ahead. Jerusalem's walls were almost 5km (3 miles) long, 3m (10ft) thick and 15m (50ft) high. Its towers were guarded by thousands of Saracen soldiers, ready to defend their city to the death. To stand any chance of breaking in, the crusaders needed siege towers – huge wheeled columns they could use to reach the top of the walls. But siege towers were made of wood, and there were few trees in that area.

The crusaders spent 39 painful days camped outside the city walls. The summer sun roasted them during the day and, at night, dry winds stung their eyes and choked their throats. The only water was a pool close to the city wall that was too dangerous to approach. Even so, many crusaders died trying, preferring to be attacked by arrows than to die of thirst.

Then, early in July 1099, two supply ships arrived at the nearby port town of Jaffa, bringing food, water – and wood. The crusaders immediately set to work. Toiling beneath the sweltering sun, they built two great siege towers, as well as huge battering rams, and giant catapults known as trebuchets.

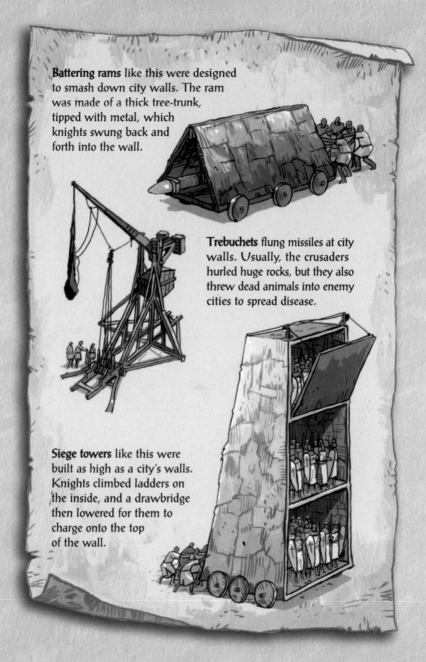

Battering rams like this were designed to smash down city walls. The ram was made of a thick tree-trunk, tipped with metal, which knights swung back and forth into the wall.

Trebuchets flung missiles at city walls. Usually, the crusaders hurled huge rocks, but they also threw dead animals into enemy cities to spread disease.

Siege towers like this were built as high as a city's walls. Knights climbed ladders on the inside, and a drawbridge then lowered for them to charge onto the top of the wall.

The siege towers were immense – giant wheeled castles, three floors high and covered in protective animal hides. As dawn rose on July 14, the crusaders began to move them towards the city walls.

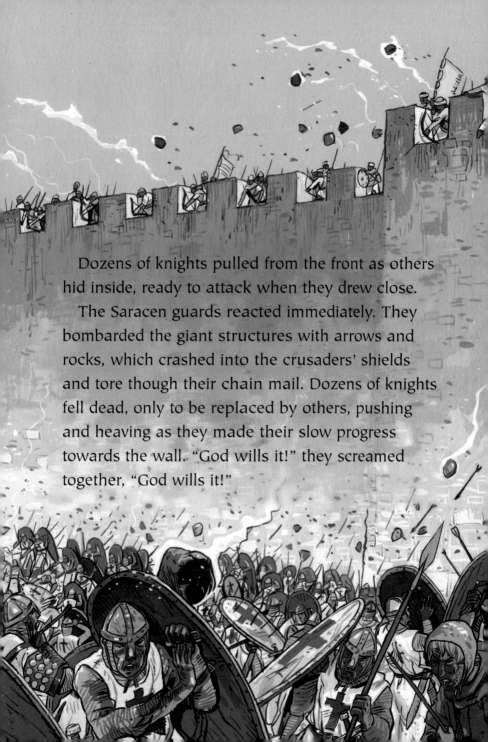

Dozens of knights pulled from the front as others
hid inside, ready to attack when they drew close.
The Saracen guards reacted immediately. They
bombarded the giant structures with arrows and
rocks, which crashed into the crusaders' shields
and tore though their chain mail. Dozens of knights
fell dead, only to be replaced by others, pushing
and heaving as they made their slow progress
towards the wall. "God wills it!" they screamed
together, "God wills it!"

Now the Saracens grew desperate. Instead of arrows, they launched lethal fire bombs at the siege engines. One of the towers was engulfed by fire, killing the knights inside. But the other one kept moving on.

Behind the tower, the attackers worked furiously to defend it. Crossbows picked out guards on the walls and catapults hurled burning bales of hay. The Saracens responded with cloud after cloud of arrows, raining down on the crusaders below.

Then, suddenly, the arrows stopped. A huge plume of smoke rose from behind the city wall. The crusaders hesitated, unsure what was happening. Then they realized: the city's guard towers were on fire. Seizing their chance, the knights swung a bridge from the siege tower to the top of the walls. Surrounded by smoke, they stormed into Jerusalem.

Charging through the city, the crusaders went wild. Innocent citizens were dragged from their houses and slaughtered in the streets. Others were burned alive in their homes. Some crusaders even fought each other as they looted and rioted through the Holy City. Their great religious crusade now ended in one of the worst massacres of the Middle Ages.

As the streets ran with blood, the leaders of the crusade gathered for a holy procession. Chanting and singing, they marched through the city to the Church of the Holy Sepulchre.

Jerusalem had been won, but the crusaders' crimes would never be forgotten. The Muslim world would have its revenge.

CHAPTER 6

The crusader kingdoms

Of the 15,000 crusaders who survived the siege of Jerusalem, only 3,000 stayed in the Holy Land. The rest returned to Europe, shattered and scarred by the experiences of the past three years. Slowly, the Holy City began to recover too. The crusaders rebuilt the city walls and chose one of their most experienced knights, Baldwin of Boulogne, to be the first King of Jerusalem.

The Holy Land was now divided into four crusader kingdoms: Jerusalem (the city and the land around it), Antioch, Edessa and Tripoli. The whole area became known as Outremer, meaning 'overseas' in French.

The crusaders enjoyed new, comfortable lives in the east. They discovered foods that were unknown in Europe, such as lemons, olives and sugar cane, and wore clothes made from luxurious new materials like cotton and silk.

The map below shows the four crusader kingdoms, as well as other places that were important during the rest of the crusades.

THE CRUSADER KINGDOMS

EDESSA

ANTIOCH

TRIPOLI

● Tiberias

● Hattin

● Acre

● Arsuf

● Jaffa

● Jerusalem

KINGDOM OF JERUSALEM

Many of the knights joined new religious military orders, groups of fighting monks dedicated to protecting the crusader kingdoms. Some of these, such as the Knights Templar and the Hospitallers, became immensely powerful, as well as incredibly rich.

The Knights Templar (in white) and Hospitaller (in black) were formed to protect Christian pilgrims visiting the Holy Land. They were elite soldiers, who fought in many battles over the next 200 years.

The crusaders also built a network of castles to protect themselves from Muslim attacks. They seemed to have settled well in their new home. But the peace was not to last.

CHAPTER 7

The Muslims fight back

By the end of the 11th century, Muslim power in the Middle East was split between three main dynasties: the Fatimids in Egypt, the Abbasids in Iraq and Seljuk Turks in the north. Had these groups combined their forces, they could easily have defeated the crusader army before it reached Jerusalem. Instead, they fought among each other, allowing the crusaders to march through the Holy Land, capturing towns and cities with little opposition.

But, in the 12th century, a new Seljuk warlord named Zengi came to power and began to unite the rival Muslim tribes. Zengi was horrified by the capture of Jerusalem and the massacre of the city's citizens by the crusaders. He dreamed of leading the entire Islamic world in a *jihad*, or holy war, against the Christians. Raising a huge army, he marched north from Syria. On Christmas Eve 1144, he captured Edessa, the weakest of the crusader kingdoms. The Muslim fightback had begun.

The Christians responded immediately. In 1145, another crusade set out from Europe, but it was a disaster. Most of the crusaders died before reaching the Holy Land. Those who survived were easily defeated by an army led by Zengi's successor, Nur ad-Din, who had sworn to continue Zengi's holy war.

When Nur ad-Din died in 1174, he was replaced by an even greater military commander – Salah ad-Din, known to the crusaders as Saladin.

Saladin had been Nur ad-Din's chief minister in Egypt, where he had gained a reputation for kindness and intelligence. But, once in power, he was determined to continue the Muslim fight against the crusaders.

In July 1187, he marched his 30,000 strong army into the Kingdom of Jerusalem and captured the crusader town of Tiberias.

As soon as he learned of the invasion, the new King of Jerusalem, Guy of Lusignan, gathered his troops and led them against Saladin in Tiberias. As they marched, they saw Saracen soldiers in the hills around them. By the time they reached a hilltop close to a town named Hattin, the crusader army was completely surrounded.

As the Saracens advanced, one of the knights fell to his knees. "Alas, Lord God," he shouted, "it is over. The Kingdom of Jerusalem is no more."

The crusaders were outnumbered and completely overwhelmed. In that one battle – at Hattin on July 4, 1187 – their entire army was destroyed. Thousands of knights lay dead on the battlefield, and thousands more were taken into slavery. Saladin had dealt them a blow from which they would never recover.

Over the next three months, Saladin tore through the Holy Land, capturing crusader towns such as Acre, Jaffa and Beruit. Then, on October 2, 1187, the great Muslim leader reached Jerusalem. But, rather than kill the Christians living there, he allowed them all to leave the city unharmed. Saladin wasn't interested in revenge; his dream had already been realized – Jerusalem was in Muslim hands once more.

CHAPTER 8

Crusade of the kings

As soon as the news reached Europe, Pope Gregory VIII immediately called for another crusade. The goal was the same – to recover Jerusalem from the Muslims – but the leaders of this new expedition were very different. Rather than nobles and knights, this third crusade would be led by kings.

The first to leave was Frederick I, the Emperor of Germany. Leading an army of 30,000, he set off from Europe in the spring of 1189. The journey was a disaster. Reaching Turkey in 1190, the 70-year-old emperor attempted to cross a river dressed in full armour. When he slipped from his horse, he drowned.

Frederick's death threw his army into chaos. Attacked by Turks, some of the soldiers fled, and others even committed suicide. The rest continued on foot, but got no further than Antioch, where most were killed by a deadly plague. The few who survived made their way to the coast, where another king, Philip II of France, had arrived.

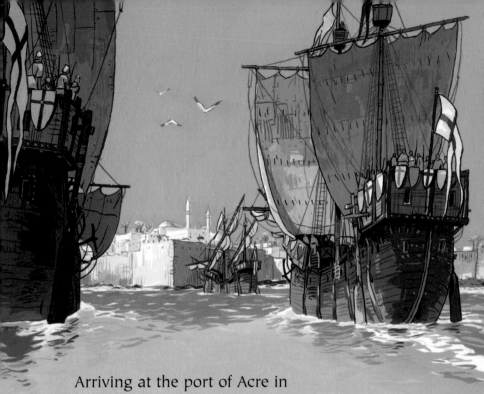

Arriving at the port of Acre in
April 1191, Philip took command of a
small crusader army that had spent the past two
years trying to recapture the city. But the French
king was little help as a military leader. Philip
hated warfare and had only joined the crusade
because it was his royal duty. He organized the
building of new siege towers, but was unable to
lead a successful attack on Acre.

Without a proper leader, things looked bleak.
Then Richard I, the king of England, arrived and
everything changed.

Richard was the complete opposite to Philip: he rode well, fought well and was a brilliant leader. He was obsessed with the crusade, and saw the capture of Jerusalem as a way to make sure he would be remembered. His courage on the battlefield had already earned him the nickname Richard the Lionheart.

As soon as he arrived in Acre, Richard took command, building more siege towers and digging beneath the city walls to weaken them. Within a month, the city had surrendered. For Richard, it was just the first taste of victory in the east. For Philip, it was enough. Exhausted, the French king returned home, leaving Richard in sole charge of the 50,000 strong crusader army.

Now Richard decided to show Saladin what he was made of. On August 20, he gathered 3,000 Muslim prisoners from Acre – men, women and children – and executed every one of them outside the city walls. By the time the slaughter was over, the ground around the city ran red with blood. Richard had sent his message to Saladin. He was coming for Jerusalem.

Two days later, Richard began his march down the coast towards Jaffa, where he hoped to launch his attack.

He knew Saladin's army would follow, and arranged his troops so that his best knights, the Templars and Hospitallers, guarded them on all sides. Richard then rode alongside his army, screaming at them to stay in position so the Saracen forces couldn't attack.

As they approached the town of Arsuf on September 7, one group of knights suddenly broke away and charged at some enemy soldiers. Richard was furious. But now his ranks were broken, he gave the order to attack.

Swirling his sword, he charged at the Saracens, driving them back with sheer force. Eventually, Saladin gave the order to retreat. He had underestimated the English king and never again dared to meet him in open battle.

Flushed with victory, Richard and his army continued to Jaffa and, by January 1192, they were within sight of Jerusalem. But the king had a new problem. He had not come to the Holy Land to stay. Even if he did capture Jerusalem, what would stop Saladin from taking it back after he left? He also received news that Philip II of France was plotting to attack his lands in Europe. Richard had to return home. Reluctantly, he asked Saladin for a truce.

In September, Richard and Saladin finally agreed on terms for peace. Jerusalem would remain under Muslim control, but Christian pilgrims would be free to visit the city again. Richard's army was the first to enter, marching unarmed through the ancient streets to pray at the Church of the Holy Sepulchre.

But Richard refused to join them. During this crusade, he had prevented Saladin from controlling the entire Holy Land by capturing the important coastal towns of Acre and Jaffa, but he had failed to liberate Jerusalem. So, instead of entering the city, he sent Saladin a warning: one day, he would be back to capture it. In reply, Saladin said that he would rather lose Jerusalem to Richard than anyone else.

But Richard never did return. On the way home, his ship was wrecked off the coast of Italy and he was taken prisoner by the German Emperor Henry VI. He was released in 1194, but died five years later from an arrow wound while leading a siege on a castle in France. The archer who fired the fatal shot was brought to the king as he lay dying. Rather than punish the soldier, Richard congratulated him on his victory, and even paid him a reward.

Saladin died earlier, in 1193. Upon his death, it was discovered that he had only one gold coin left in his purse. He'd spent all the money he had on his war to recover Jerusalem.

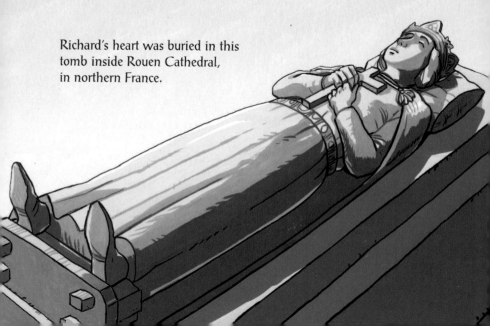

Richard's heart was buried in this tomb inside Rouen Cathedral, in northern France.

CHAPTER 9

The last crusades

Over almost 200 years, between 1096 and 1271, there were a total of nine crusades. But during the 13th century, the expeditions were motivated more and more by greed rather than religion. Capturing Jerusalem was no longer the goal. Instead, ambitious knights used the crusades to gain wealth or steal land.

Some people, though, still dreamed of Jerusalem. In 1212, twenty thousand children embarked on a crusade led by a boy who claimed to see visions of God. But none of them ever reached the east – most died of starvation, and the rest were taken into slavery in Italy.

By the end of the 13th century, Jerusalem remained under Muslim control. One by one the other crusader towns of Outremer were reconquered by Muslim armies. But the crusaders made other gains. Their experiences in the Holy Land taught them a lot about eastern forms of medicine, mathematics and astronomy. Trade with the east increased too, and luxurious new products such as silk and spices began to enter Europe.

As demand for these items increased, European traders looked for other places around the world to find them. Launching their ships, they set off in search of new lands to conquer.

Timeline of the crusades

1071-1095 - Turks invade the Holy Land, capturing Jerusalem.

27 November 1095 - Pope Urban II calls for a crusade to recover the Holy City.

Spring 1096 - The Peasants' Crusade sets off from Europe - and is easily defeated six months later, in Turkey.

1096 -1099 - An army of crusader knights, often known as the First Crusade, marches to Jerusalem. On July 1, they defeat a Saracen army in the Battle of Dorylaeum.

7 June 1099 - Crusader army reaches Jerusalem, and capture the city on July 14. The Holy Land is divided into four 'crusader kingdoms', known together as Outremer.

1144 - Zengi captures the crusader kingdom of Edessa. In 1145, his successor Nur ad-Din defeats the Second Crusade.

July 4, 1187 - Saladin defeats the crusaders at the Battle of Hattin, then recaptures Jerusalem on October 2.

1189 - A third crusade marches from Europe to recover the Holy City.

1191 - Richard I captures Acre, then defeats Saladin at the Battle of Arsuf on 7 September.

September 1192 - Unable to capture Jerusalem, Richard agrees a peace treaty with Saladin.

13th century - Several more crusades are launched from Europe, but they achieve little. Jerusalem remains in Muslim hands.

Index

Designed by Andrea Slane
Edited by Jane Chisholm

First published in 2007 by Usborne Publishing Ltd,
Usborne House, 83-85 Saffron Hill, London EC1N 8RT, England. www.usborne.com